THE DISASTROUS LITTLE DRAGON

GILLIAN JOHNSON

For Vi

The whole thing started with a sneeze.
And before you could say ...

... four sneezy snufflers:

Carolyn Rutherford

Tom Dunn

Dylan Whipple

and

Sylvie Spark

– who also happened to be the naughtiest children in the school – were placed in quarantine at Sister Winifred's house,

where they were told:

You must
NOT, UNDER ANY
CIRCUMSTANCES,
OPEN THAT MEDICINE
CABINET.

But the children were little monsters.

'GIVE THEM BACK!'

Sylvie snatched Tom's glasses, so he threw his book at her, but missed and hit the medicine cabinet ...

... that turned out to be a door to

another world.

And the castle
in the other world
turned out to be

a hospital for sick and injured

MONSTERS ...

... where Carolyn, Tom, Sylvie and Dylan were handed lab coats. 'Get to work, doctors!'

'DOCTORS?

But we're too YOUNG!'

'IT TAKES A MONSTER
TO KNOW A MONSTER!
THAT MAKES YOU CHILDREN
MORE THAN QUALIFIED!'

FLAP FLAP

'No time to waste, doctors!'

Because flying through the door that very moment were two of the smokiest dragons the children had ever seen.

'Help him,' cried the big dragon.

The little dragon's wings were charred. His nostrils were filled with soot. He opened his mouth to speak but only smoke came out. Then he **coughed** and **coughed** and **coughed** and **coughed**.

'STOP THAT, BARTHOLOMEW!' roared the big dragon.

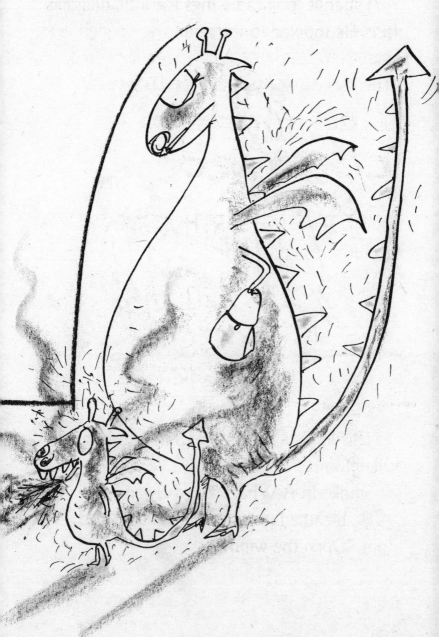

A strange look came over the little dragon's face. He toppled to the floor.

'This looks like a case of Smoke Inhalation!' cried Tom.

'Smoke-In-A-What?' asked Dylan.

'He breathed in too much smoke!' said Tom. 'Open the windows!'

'Find the Smoke Buster Mask!' screeched
Carolyn.

'Get the crackle berry syrup!' ordered Sylvie.

The doctors laid the little dragon on the
bench in the Quiet Room.

'Open wide!' said Sylvie.

The dragon refused.

'Open your mouth!' roared the big dragon.

'Are you his mother?' asked Sylvie.

'No, I'm his aunty Madge,' said the big dragon. 'I have taken care of him since he was an egg. He has always been a problem!'

'What happened to him?' asked Sylvie.
'Was there a fire?'

'I wish!' cried Madge, shoving the doctors aside and wrenching open Bartholomew's mouth.

His teeth were small, sharp and dirty.
'His tongue's purple!' cried Dylan.
There was a pile of grey ash at the
back of his throat.

Sylvie put on a
pair of rubber gloves

and swept
out the ash.

Bartholomew
sputtered.
His breath
smelled like
burnt bacon.

Tom fitted the Smoke Buster Mask and
Dylan scrubbed Bartholomew with a sponge.

Sylvie faced Madge.

'Where did all the **SMOKE** come from?'
'From *Bartholomew*, stupid girl,' said Madge.
'He made it himself?' asked Sylvie.
'Yes. He is ten years old and instead of making flames, he makes smoke.

THERE IS SOMETHING VERY WRONG WITH MY NEPHEW!'

Silence fell. Madge's heavy breathing was making the room very hot.

Finally Tom spoke. 'Proper dragons should be able to blow flames by the age of ten.'

Madge nodded. 'All of Bartholomew's cousins could breathe fire by the age of *eight*. Now they are protecting princesses as proper dragons should!

'I have tried everything! Tutors! Special diet!
Nothing works. He won't focus. *And* his
flying is rubbish! He'll *never* be a **proper
dragon!**'

Bartholomew trembled.

The crackle berry syrup will help!

'Yes, where is it?'

'Carolyn drank it on one of her midnight feasts!'

'It was our only supply!'

'It wasn't MY fault! Someone stored it in the Maple Syrup Bottle!'

'But I needed the jar for my science experiment.'

Madge

SNORTED

with rage.

'You call yourselves **doctors**? You don't even have the right medicine!'

At that moment, Carolyn returned holding up a frosted tub. 'Madagascar vanilla ice cream!' she announced.

Bartholomew sat up smiling.

The room grew very, very **HOT**.

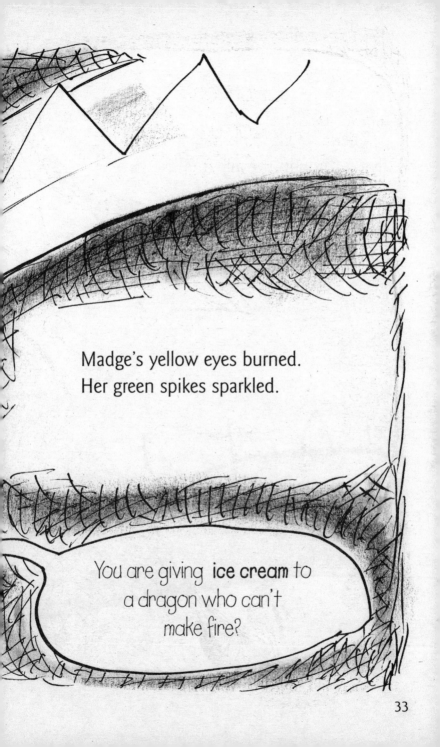

Madge's yellow eyes burned.
Her green spikes sparkled.

You are giving **ice cream** to
a dragon who can't
make fire?

Then she lifted her tail and sent the tub flying through the air.

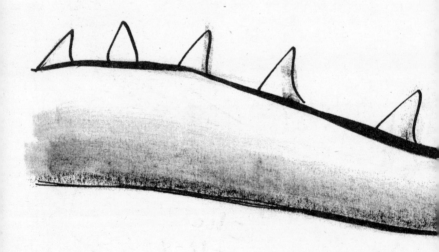

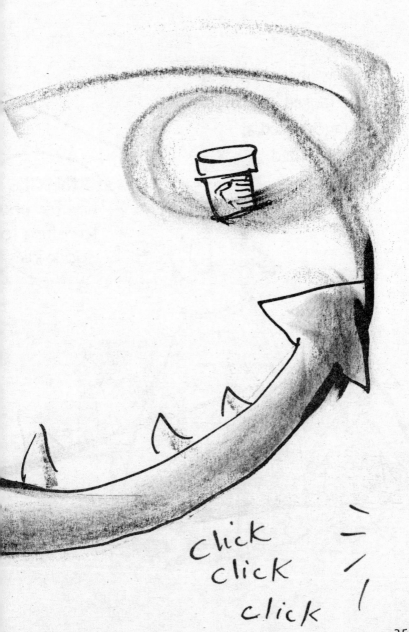

click
click
click

35

It was Sister Winifred!
She looked at Madge.
Madge looked at
Sister Winifred.

I think it's time for you to return to your lair.

Sister Winifred smiled. 'He'll be in good hands,' she said. 'Now off you go.'

'But I don't want Bartholomew eating ice cream, it's junk food. Besides, he's never spent a night away from home,' said Madge.

'There's a first time for everything,' said Sister Winifred cheerfully.

'I'll be back first
thing tomorrow,
Bartholomew,'
promised Madge.
'With your special
breakfast. And a
clean vest. And
your cod liver oil!'

39

With Madge gone, the children turned their attention to solving the mystery.

They removed the Smoke Buster Mask and got to work.

Tom took XRAYS.

'Though his wings are on the small side,' Tom added.

Sylvie collected burps ...

... and other important gases

which she tested in the lab using a
Bunsen Burner.

'All normal!' she said.

Tom explained their findings.

'When Bartholomew breathes in air, his fire gland revs up and produces a methane gas mist. When the mist is concentrated it turns into sparks. The sparks make fire.

'Most dragons, by the age of ten, can make fire whenever they want simply by breathing in deeply and blowing out. All of Bartholomew's results are normal. He **should** be able to blow flames.'

Tom crossed his arms. 'Maybe we're missing something.'

'The crackle berry syrup!' groaned Sylvie. 'That's what we're missing!'

Tom and Sylvie went back to the lab to write their reports.

Carolyn and Dylan wheeled the patient to the room where he would spend the night.

They plumped his pillows and tucked him in.
'Are you afraid?' asked Carolyn.

'No,' said Bartholomew.

'Do you have a best friend?' asked Dylan.

'No.'

'Your aunty said you have never spent the night away.'

'I'm not allowed sleepovers,' Bartholomew shrugged.

'You didn't bring in a toy,' said Dylan.

'I don't have any,' said Bartholomew grumpily. 'Aunty Madge scorched my pet rocks when I failed my last flame test.'

Carolyn tried not to be shocked.

'Why is your aunty so mean to you?'
Bartholomew began to grind his teeth.
There are only so many questions a dragon
can answer before he has to ...

blow a little **SMOKE**.

The air turned
GOOPY and **GREY**.

Coughing, the two doctors opened the
windows and staggered out of the dragon's
room.

The truth was, Bartholomew *was* scared. And he was very sad, too. Maybe Aunty Madge was right. He would never be a **proper dragon**.

In the middle of the night,
Bartholomew woke up,
SHIVERING.

Aunty always yelled at
him when he woke in the
middle of the night.

GO BACK
Bartho
DON't
concen

to BEd

lomew

eat that!

trate !

But there were no shouts.

No orders from Aunty Madge.
Just silence.

With the smoke cleared from the room, Bartholomew's sense of smell had returned.

A delicious odour was wafting into his room.

He tiptoed toward it.

It felt good to move. He tested his wings and was surprised to feel them lifting him up out of the room ...

and down the dark corridor. His wings were
not working perfectly yet ...

so he bumped into the walls and hit his head on the ceiling.

He didn't care. I felt good to follow the delicious smell down the crumbly stairs . . .

He didn't care. It felt good to follow the
delicious smell down the crumbly stairs ...

... to the kitchen. Bartholomew's
mouth watered.

His stomach rumbled. Then ...

65

What was **that**?
There was no time to think.

He jumped into the drawer where he
fitted snugly between two large tubs. The

ICE CREAM FREEZER!

Cold yes, but not unpleasant. Outside,
he could hear something shuffling around.

He would wait here until it stopped.
He lifted the lid and sampled.

Yum!

The ice cream tasted so good that
Bartholomew didn't notice the legs walking
towards him.

His mouth was too stuffed with ice cream
to yell, 'STOP!'

But nobody could hear him. He was locked inside the freezer!

Several hours later, Carolyn returned to the kitchen for her usual midnight feast.

The odd sounds she'd heard earlier were gone.

The coast was clear and she was starving!

She opened the freezer door and reached for the ice cream.

She examined her arm. A graze ran from her wrist to her elbow.

WHAT WAS THAT?

She was wide awake now. She peered into the freezer.

There, furred over with ice crystals, was the little dragon.

'Bartholomew?'

But Bartholomew did not reply.
He did not move either!
His legs and tail were stiff.

HE WAS FROZEN SOLID!

She dragged him out of the
freezer, across the kitchen floor ...

and up the crumbly stairs ...

... to her bedroom where she placed him on her bed and carefully scraped the frost off his scales.

Then she changed into her nightgown and crawled into bed beside him.

'Maybe the best treatment for a frozen dragon is a cuddle,' she said.

At dawn Bartholomew woke up. Where was he?

Who was the girl beside him with the long blonde hair?

She looked like the princesses that his cousins had described.

The girl opened her eyes and sat up.

'You rescued me,' said Bartholomew.

'True,' said Carolyn.

'Are you a princess?' asked Bartholomew.

Carolyn ran her fingers through her hair.

She fluttered her eyes.

'Yes, Bart. I suppose you could say I am.'

Bartholomew gazed at her wonderingly.

'No one has ever called me
Bart before,' he said.

No one has ever called me princess before, except Mummy of course.

'You can protect me,' teased Carolyn. 'Just like a proper dragon would.' She was very relieved that Bartholomew was OK.

Or was he?

Suddenly Bartholomew's wings drooped.

A tear rolled down his cheek.

'You should be happy!' cried Carolyn. 'You're not frozen any more!'

Bartholomew shook his head. 'I can't protect you! I'm not –I'll never be – a **proper dragon**.'

Carolyn paced back and forth.

She stopped. The blood drained from her face.
The crackle berry syrup!

'I drank the medicine that would make you
better! That would let you blow fire!'

'Huh?' said Bartholomew.

'We need more crackle berries. But they grow very far away. By the edge of the Vast Volcano.'

'Where is that?' asked Bartholomew.

'Farther than we can walk. Farther than we can see ...'

Carolyn turned to him, remembering Madge's words.

'And farther than you can fly ...'

Bartholomew gulped.

He did not want to admit that the journey
to the freezer had been the longest flight he'd
made using his own wings. He took a very
deep breath.

'No it's not!'
he cried.
'Really?'
asked Carolyn.
'Are you sure?'

'Yes,' said Bartholomew
bravely. 'I can do it!'
'Then wait here! I need
to find something. I'll
be right back!'
Carolyn
dashed to
Dylan's
room ...

... and borrowed the jar he used to store his pet nits, which had been the original crackle berry jar.

Bartholomew was waiting by the window.

They were off to a bumpy start.

They circled the castle three times ...

'I'M DIzzzzzY!'

skimmed the moat ...

SPLASH

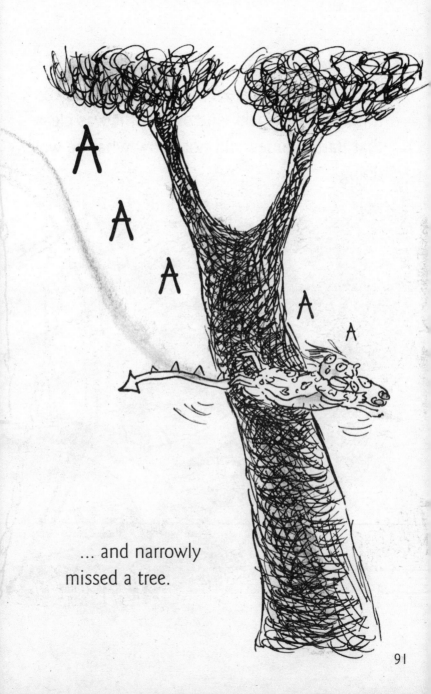

... and narrowly
missed a tree.

Carolyn was scared. What HAD she been thinking? 'Go back!' she ordered. It was clear that Bartholomew did not know what he was doing!

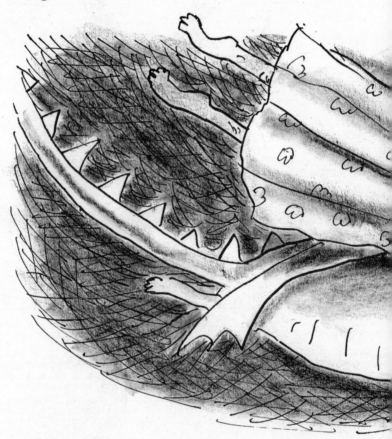

Bartholomew refused.

'Then use both wings!' cried Carolyn.
'I'll steer!'

It worked!

He straightened out. His wings stretched wide. His power surged. Across the Thick Wood they flew, over hills and rivers ...

... to the edge of the Vast Volcano where the crackle berries grew.

In no time at all they had filled the nit jar.

Meanwhile ...
Things were not going well back at the castle.

Madge was about to arrive but nobody knew where Bartholomew or Carolyn had disappeared to.

Tom, Sylvie and Dylan held an emergency meeting in Bartholomew's room. 'Let's call Sister Winifred,' said Dylan. 'She'll know what to do!'

'No,' said Sylvie. 'We'll do this ourselves!'

Then, to their astonishment, the window burst open.

'To the Vast Volcano!' said Carolyn.
'What's in the jar?' demanded Sylvie.
'Fresh crackle berries!' cried Carolyn. 'We picked them ourselves!'

'You took your patient to that dangerous place?' asked Sylvie.

'No. He took me!' said Carolyn.

'You,' sputtered Sylvie, 'are a disgrace to the medical establishment!'

Bartholomew did not like the way Sylvie spoke.

'Bart will protect the princess!' he growled.

'Carolyn? A princess?' said Dylan. 'Now I've heard everything!'

Bartholomew flicked his tail. Though small, he no longer looked dumpy.

104

He **GROWLED**.

A shower of sparks spewed from his mouth. Tom, Sylvie and Dylan backed away.

Something was different.

BART!

It was Carolyn who put a stop to the standoff.

'Bart, turn around and look at me. What Dylan says is actually true. I'm no princess. I'm just one of them.'

Bartholomew shook his head. 'No,' he said.

'Let me prove it,' said Carolyn, dashing out the door.

When she returned a few minutes later, she was wearing her lab coat with her hair tied in pigtails.

Bartholomew took one look and his wings sagged.

Once more he resembled a pudding.

'You don't look anything like a princess now,' he said.

At that moment, louder than a smoke alarm, Madge flapped in, carrying an overnight bag in her arms.

'I've been searching every room. Where were you all? What is Bartholomew doing out of bed? I hope you haven't served him junk food! Bartholomew?

Your high-fibre cereal ...

Now look
here.

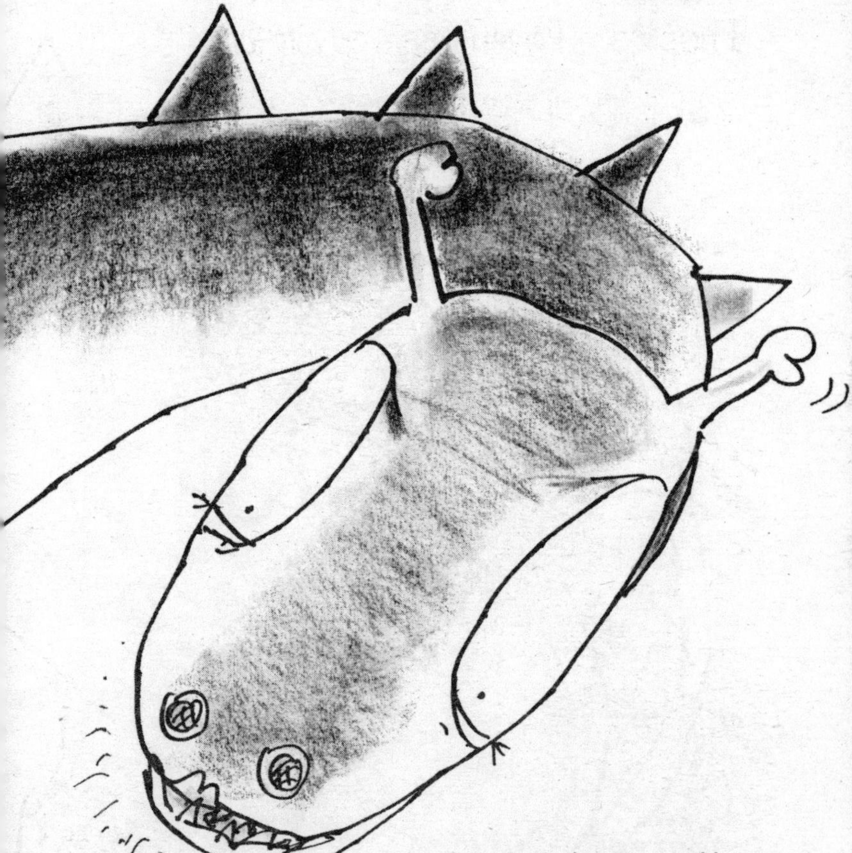

... and a clean vest!
When you have eaten,
you can put it on.
It's so cold in this castle!'

'And of course we mustn't forget your cod liver oil! A double dose I think, yah?'

A DOUBLE DOSE OF
COD LIVER OIL???

Bartholomew had had enough.
He let out a loud burp.
But what followed surprised them all ...

A ten-foot flame **whooshed** out
of Bartholomew's mouth

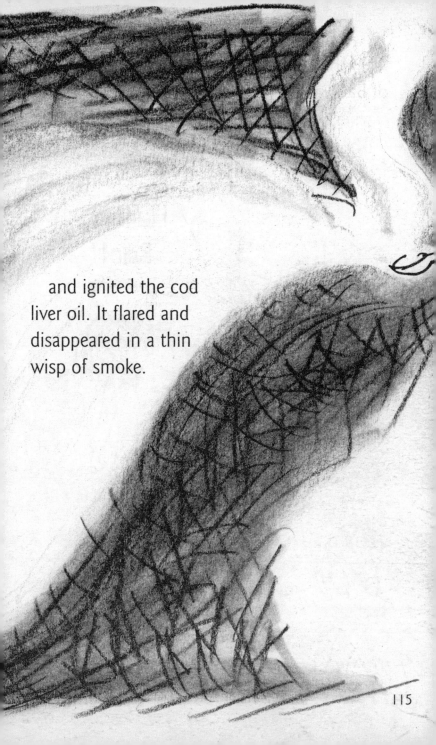

and ignited the cod
liver oil. It flared and
disappeared in a thin
wisp of smoke.

Bartholomew's first flame! He had done it all by himself, without any help from the crackle berries.

The children celebrated.

Hurrah, Bart!

Madge stared at her nephew as if seeing him for the first time.

BARTHOLOMEW?

117

Bartholomew wasn't listening.

'Bartholomew,' he said forcefully, 'is no name for a **PROPER DRAGON**. From now on, you will call me **BART**.'

Madge gulped. 'Yes, Bart. Of course.' She turned to the children. 'I told you he had it in him!' she said.

It was Sister Winifred!
She passed around bowls of ice cream.
'100% organic,' she promised.

Then Madge and Bart gathered their things and flew out of the castle window, across the moat, under the trees and back to their lair, where dragons belong.

Sister Winifred turned to Tom, Dylan, Sylvie and Carolyn. She smiled broadly. 'Now I am sure you are all in a rush to return to school...'

And that was good because coming into their emergency room that very moment was a ...

Turn the page to read about how Sylvie, Dylan, Carolyn and Tom deal with a Big Fat Smelly Ogre!

'Doctors! Your patient needs you!'
Sister Winifred called. 'Or perhaps I made
a mistake when I chose you for the job ...
perhaps you are not the little monsters that
I thought you were?'

She handed them a clipboard.

'Then go into the Quiet Room with this, and ask your monster questions! Find out who he is! What's wrong with him! How you can help him!'

The two girls took the clipboard ...

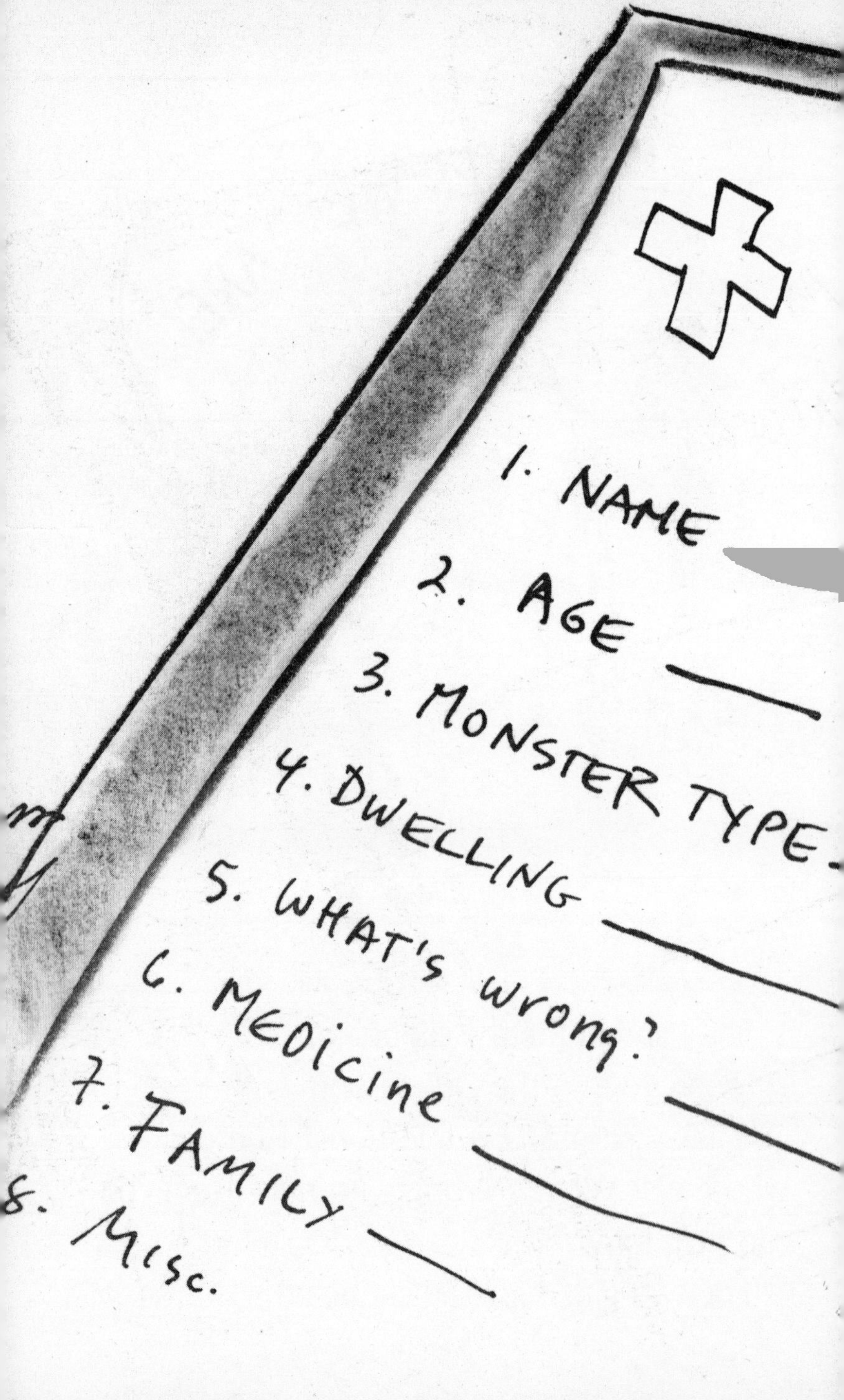

1. NAME _____

2. AGE _____

3. MONSTER TYPE _____

4. DWELLING _____

5. WHAT's wrong? _____

6. MEDicine _____

7. FAMILY _____

8. Misc.

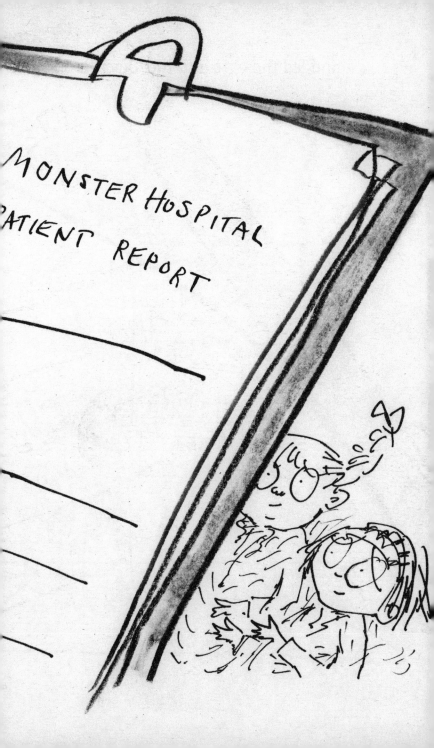

... and led the ogre into the Quiet Room.

'What's your name, ogre?' asked Sylvie.

'Frank,' replied the ogre.

'How old are you?'
'About fourteen.'

'Where do you live?'
'In a cave. In the Thick Wood.'

'How did you get here?'
'Me seven-mile boots brung me,' said Frank.

'And when did this ... flatulence start?'
asked Sylvie.
'Huh?'

'She means the farts,' added Carolyn.
Frank scowled.

There are only so many questions a sick
ogre can answer, before he needs to ...

Fart!

Hodder
Children's
Books

Turn the page

for more fantastic fiction

from Hodder Children's Books ...

Stone Goblins

Tree Goblin

Puddle Goblin

GOBLINS

By David Melling

Shadow Goblin

Ghost Goblin

GOBLINS

By David Melling

The land of the goblins is hidden, but not so far away.
If you look carefully, you might just find it!

The Goblins series is written and illustrated by the
bestselling creator of **HUGLESS DOUGLAS**, David Melling.

Check out **www.hiddengoblins.co.uk** for more
Goblins information and activities.

Hodder
Children's
Books

CLAUDE

Claude is no ordinary dog – he's the coolest canine on the block! With his faithful sidekick Sir Bobblysock, he leads an extraordinary life of the greatest adventures!

'A wonderful creation for newly independent readers.'
– The Bookseller

www.hodderchildrens.co.uk